COCO'S F...
Changing Climate Anxiety into Climate Action

By: Jeremy D. Wortzel & Lena K. Champlin
And the Group for the Advancement of Psychiatry - Climate Committee

Illustrated By: Lena K. Champlin

First Published in the United States
by Future Perfect.Media LLC in 2021

ISBN: 978-0-578-98972-3

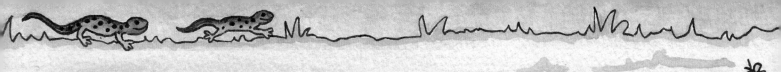

Acknowledgments

Special thanks to Joshua R. Wortzel for his help with conceptualization, content development, and manuscript editing.

Group for the Advancement of Psychiatry (GAP) - Climate Committee

Elizabeth Haase, MD (Co-Chair): American Psychiatric Association Committee on Climate Change and Mental Health, Chair; University of Nevada at Reno School of Medicine, Associate Professor of Psychiatry; Carson Tahoe Regional Medical Center, Medical Director of Psychiatry

Janet Lewis, MD (Co-Chair): University of Rochester, Clinical Assistant Professor of Psychiatry

Beth Mark, MD, MES: University of Pennsylvania Counseling and Psychological Services, Staff Psychiatrist

Joshua R. Wortzel, MD, MPhil: American Psychiatric Association Committee on Climate Change and Mental Health, Member; University of Rochester, Co-Chief Resident Psychiatrist

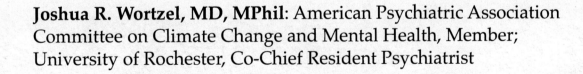

For Coco, Pine Park was perfect because
It was home and she loved it just as it was.

One day Papa Pecan got mail from his sister
Who said that a fire in her forest just missed her!

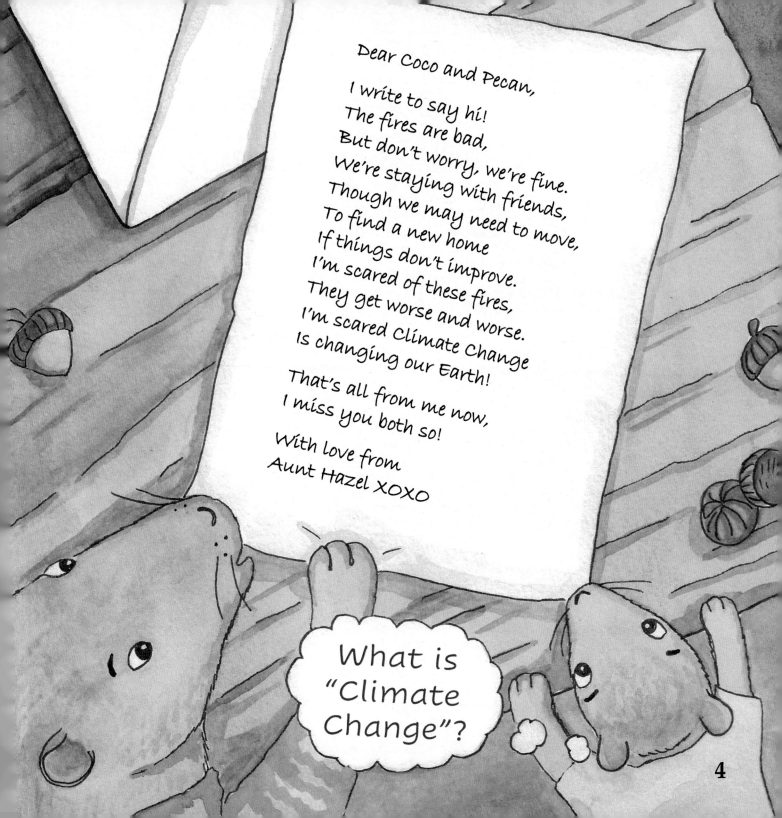

At lunch, little Coco
could not eat at all...

... or even play catch with
her acorn-shaped ball.

She ran to her room and
slammed shut the door,
but didn't quite know what
she did all that for.

Poor Coco felt worried, her legs felt like jelly
She felt like those fires were inside her belly.

6

"My dear, are you sad? Would you like us to chat?"
Papa Pecan soon asked as he came in and sat.

"I'm scared!" Coco cried. "And something feels wrong.
I'm feeling a fire that doesn't belong."

"That fire you feel is worry right now,
But it can be changed, and I'll show you how."

8

"Let's first clear your head
to get worries out.
Pretend it's your birthday.
Blow candles - let's count."

"First take a deep breath."

"Now hold it in tight."

"Then blow it all out,
with all of your might."

And then papa asked, "What's the cause of your fear?"
She whimpered, "The climate is changing right here!"

"Well, Climate Change *can* be scary for all!
Let's learn what to do. I've a friend we can call!"

"Meet good Dr. Hoot in her laboratory.
She studies the climate and will tell us the story."

"What *is* Climate Change?" Coco asked with a plea.
"I'll show you a chart that really helps me."

"The Earth has a blanket that keeps temperatures right.
But we add more blankets using oil for light."

"This changes the weather, it changes a lot
Getting stormy and cold or dry and quite hot."

"Then what," Coco asked, "can make it all stop?
I want us to stop adding blankets on top!"

"We now need to treat the Earth with respect,
And use much less oil to help and protect."

14

Papa Pecan asked Coco as they walked through the park,
"Has your worrying fire become a new spark?"

"I get Climate Change. I'm feeling less scared.
But what can I do? Are there others who care?"

"Oh, you're not alone. There are others you'll find.
There, look! Pepper Possum and kids holding signs!"

"Hi Pepper, what's up? Are you busy today?"
"Come march about Climate! We've something to say!"

By joining the group, Coco learned things to do.
Like wind power helps to stop Climate Change too.

4

17

"Let's stop using oil!" Coco eagerly cried.
And Coco could feel something changing inside.

18

Next day, with her dad, as they walked to her school
She said, "You know, Dad, now my fire feels cool!"

"It started off hot and scary and red
But now it feels blue and exciting instead."

At school where she learned how to write her own letter,
She had an idea that could make the world better.

How to ...e a l
- Gree
- Par
- signa

"Let's write to our leaders to tell them we care
About Climate Change and the Earth that we share!"

As Coco wrote notes asking leaders to help,
Her fire found words to match how she felt.

Her fire then pushed her to Pine City Hall.
"Please listen, Judge Jelly, to our warning call!"

"I hear you now, Coco, and I'm lending a paw,
We'll all use less oil with my wind-power law."

Next week when they walked through the park Papa asked,
"Are you feeling okay? There's a lot changing fast."

PINE PARK
PASSES WIND!

"I feel good for Pine Park, but what of the rest?
The whole world's in danger. Do others feel stressed?"

At that very moment, Sunny Songbird arrived.
"Hey, how was your flight?" Coco happily cried.

"I flew from afar where we all met together.
We're saving the planet – every paw, fin, and feather."

24

"For climate connection across the world too,
I bring news from some creatures
who care just like you."

Coco had an idea, "I've a note I should write."
And Sunny said, "Great! I'll send it tonight."

25

Dear Aunt Hazel Nut,

I write to say hey!
Those fires sound scary,
I'm glad you're okay.
Though Climate Change seems
So big and unknown,
I want you to know
That you're never alone.
See creatures care lots,
All over the globe.
They're changing their worries
To actions and hope.
The things they are doing
Can help bring about
A healthier Climate
And keep fires out.
Let's join to save Earth
We've got lots to do!

Love Coco P. Nut,
And Papa Nut too

Then Papa leaned in, "How's your worry flame doing?
By joining this work, are your worries improving?"

"I'm feeling good now - my flame doesn't fret.
It's helping me get more involved, not upset."

28

At home in Pine Park, the sun slowly set
What a beautiful place to love and protect.

6

And Coco now knew how to change her scared fire,
From a flame causing worry to a friend who inspires.

30

Resources for Caregivers

Look for the acorn symbols throughout the book that relate to these additional resources

 ## What is Climate Anxiety? (pg. 6)

Climate anxiety is a term that is being used to describe the worries, uncertainty, and stress felt about global Climate Change. Many people struggle with this crisis, though children and young adults may be particularly vulnerable. Introducing the topic of Climate Change to young children is important to help them develop emotional resources and a factual understanding of climate events to which they are already exposed. This book aims to help children channel their anxiety into action and agency and to model how adults can help children navigate this challenging process.

 ## Getting the Worries Out (pg. 9)

There are many coping and grounding techniques that children can learn to help manage anxiety. Here we introduce a deep breathing technique, but please try others as well:
www.apa.org/topics/child-development/stress

Addressing Climate Anxiety: "The Climate Talk"

In this book, we structure "The Climate Talk" into a 6-point, evidence-based framework to avoid common misconceptions that may contribute to more anxiety.

1 Setting the stage (pg. 10): Try to find a quite space to chat and sit at eye level. Begin the conversation with asking what the child knows about Climate Change.

2 Teaching Climate Change (pg. 12): Decrease the mystery of Climate Change and explain the science in simple, clear language: climatekids.nasa.gov/menu/teach/

3 Feeling a part of a community (pg. 16 & 24): When discussing the work that needs to be done to prevent Climate Change, it is important to show children that they are joining a thriving local and global community already working towards this goal.

4 Taking action and getting involved (pg. 17): Learn about impactful ways that children can get involved: kidsagainstclimatechange.co/

5 Encouraging future conversations (pg. 28): Set the stage for more conversations on this topic. Addressing anxiety is a process rather than a one-and-done conversation.

6 Inspiring natural wonder (pg. 29): An important way to inspire children to connect with and protect the Earth is to get them outside: generationwild.com/get-kids-outside

Made in the USA
Middletown, DE
27 October 2022